Lalaloopsy

Sew Magical! Sew Cute!™

Party Time!

by Lauren Cecil

SCHOLASTIC INC.

New York   Toronto   London   Auckland   Sydney   Mexico City   New Delhi   Hong Kong

ISBN 978-0-545-37998-4

12

14 15 16 / 0

Designed by Angela Jun
Printed in the U.S.A.
First printing, September 2011

40

Jewel Sparkles was going to visit her friend Crumbs Sugar Cookie. Crumbs was the best baker in Lalaloopsy Land. Jewel couldn't wait to taste Crumbs' newest creation!

"**W**ell, what do you think?" Crumbs asked. "I just perfected my recipe for strawberry-surprise cupcakes."

"Mmmm. These are your best yet!" Jewel said. "I have an idea. What if we threw a party and invited all our friends? That way everyone could taste your yummy cupcakes."

"Great idea!" Crumbs agreed. "Maybe our friends would want to help us plan the party, too."

Crumbs and Jewel's first stop was Bea Spells-a-Lot's house. "Hi, Bea. Guess what?" Crumbs said. "We're planning a party!"

"I love parties. And I love to write," said Bea. She also liked to talk a lot. "I can make invitations and a fun sign, too."

Next, Jewel and Crumbs went to see Peanut Big Top.
"Hi, Peanut!" Jewel said. "We're having a party. Want to come?"
"I love parties," Peanut said. "Could I put on a show?"
"What a delicious idea!" Crumbs replied.

Jewel and Crumbs visited Pillow Featherbed next.
"Pillow, wake up," said Crumbs gently. "We're planning a party.
Is there anything you'd like to bring?"

Pillow yawned. Then she said, "I can bring some fluffy cushions
so everyone has a comfy seat."

"Fantastic!" Jewel said.

Next Crumbs and Jewel went to Dot Starlight's house. "Do you like this song?" Dot cried over the loud music.

"Definitely! It will be perfect for the party we're planning!" Jewel said.

"Sounds like a blast." Dot said, "I can't wait!"

ewel and Crumbs went to see Spot Splatter Splash next. "We're planning a party!" Jewel said. "Since you're such a great artist, maybe you could make some decorations?"

"Of course!" Spot said. "I've got lots of creative ideas!"

"Jewel, we almost forgot about you!" Crumbs said. "What would you like to bring to the party?"

"I like to dress up for parties. So I'm going to make everyone a glittery tiara!" said Jewel.

"Great idea!" Crumbs said.

Their last stop was Mittens Fluff 'n' Stuff's house.

"Hi, Mittens. We're planning a party!" Crumbs said.

"What can I do to help?" Mittens asked.

"Whatever you're good at," Jewel replied. "I like to dress up for parties, so I'm making tiaras."

"And I love to bake, so I'm making cupcakes," Crumbs explained. "I like snowflakes, icicles, and flurries. But I can't bring those to a party," Mittens said. "Maybe I'll just help you instead."

Crumbs tried to teach Mittens how to make cupcakes. But Mittens' cupcakes didn't come out quite right.

"I'm not as good at baking as you are," Mittens said sadly. "Maybe I'll help with Jewel's tiaras instead."

Jewel showed Mittens how to decorate tiaras, but Mittens' tiaras didn't come out quite as nice as Jewel's.

"I'm no good at making tiaras either!" Mittens cried as she ran home. "I'll be the only one who didn't help with the party!"

glue

Jewel and Crumbs found Mittens at her house. She was very upset.
"Everyone has a special talent but me," Mittens sniffed.
"That's not true, Mittens," said Crumbs.
"You're great at lots of things," said Jewel.

"I'm great at building snowmen, but I can't bring a snowman to the party. . . . Wait a minute — that's it! *Snow!*"

Jewel and Crumbs looked at each other. "Huh?"

"I'll explain later," said Mittens. "I've got a great idea!"

"Looks like everything is ready," Spot said as she put the finishing touches on the decorations.

"But we are missing one very important thing — " Crumbs added. "Mittens!"

"I hope she comes," Peanut agreed. "It just wouldn't be the same without her."

PARTY TiMe!

Just then, someone knocked at the door.
"Mittens!" Jewel cried. "You came!"

"I sure did! And I brought an extra-special treat," Mittens said proudly.

"**W**ould you like to try my triple-mint snow cones?" Mittens asked. "Absolutely," Crumbs exclaimed. Then she took a bite. "Yum! No one could have made these better than you!"

Because everyone worked together, the party was a hit! Bea's invitations let everyone know where to go. Spot's decorations made the party look cheerful, and all the girls looked festive because of Jewel's beautiful tiaras.

paRTy TiMe!

The girls danced to Dot's music. Then they watched Peanut put on a juggling show.

Finally, the girls sat back on the cushions that Pillow brought and snacked on Crumbs' cupcakes and Mittens' snow cones.

"This was the best party ever!" Mittens said when the party was over. "I had so much fun."

"And your snow cones were a hit!" Crumbs said.

"They're cool," Jewel added. "*And* sweet — just like you!"